Phoebe and the River Flute

BY M. C. HELLDORFER

ILLUSTRATED BY PAUL HESS

A Doubleday Book for Young Readers

A Doubleday Book for Young Readers
Published by
Random House, Inc.
1540 Broadway
New York, New York 10036

Cataloging-in-Publication Data is available from the Library of Congress.
ISBN: 0-385-32338-7

The text of this book is set in 18-point Garamond No. 3.
Book design by Trish Parcell Watts
Manufactured in the United States of America
March 2000
10 9 8 7 6 5 4 3 2 1
WOR

For Cindy and Bina
M.C.H.

For Kerine
P.H.

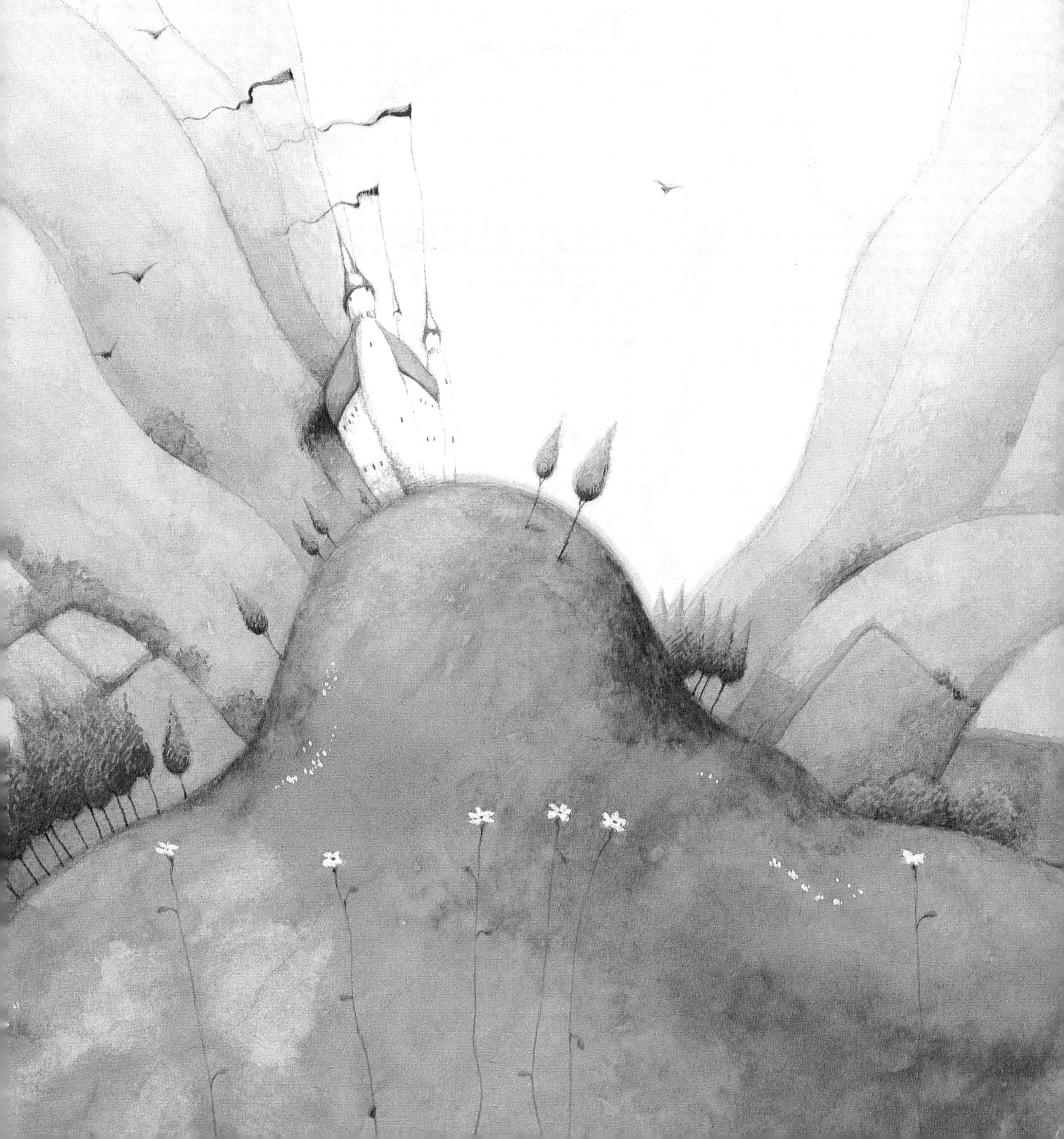

$\mathcal{L}$ong ago there was a garden with walls that towered high as the trees, where vines climbed up leaf upon leaf, petal upon petal, to spread a canopy of flowers far above. Inside the garden lived one hundred rare and beautiful birds. A girl named Phoebe cared for them.

She lived in the garden and, from the time she was young, understood the songs of the captive birds. Each one had taught her its secret name. Hearing the girl's silvery whistling, they always came. Phoebe, who had no family, loved them as her own.

But the birds had been collected by a king, and the garden belonged to his son. The prince was the same age as Phoebe and came there to play. One day they made swings from the vines. Together they soared high as two birds, till the twisting leaves pulled them back to earth again.

Phoebe and the prince often talked of the land they glimpsed beyond the garden wall. Both dreamed of exploring the distant river. Then one spring the old king died. The prince set off for lands beyond the river, leaving Phoebe and the kingdom in the hands of his uncle.

This uncle was feared by many, for he was a man whose only joy was power over others. Under his rule, Phoebe was never allowed to leave the garden. "Better to lose your hand, girl, than one of our royal birds," the old man would threaten.

For three long years no one heard from the prince. Phoebe wished she could see her friend again. What birds had he discovered? she wondered. How did wild creatures soar when they were free?

Phoebe opened the garden gate to gaze out at the faraway river. Suddenly there was a flutter of wings. While she was dreaming, a bird escaped from the garden—the prince's favorite! Quickly Phoebe closed the gate and followed the bird, calling its name softly. But the bird, finding the wide sky open to it, cried back one last time and flew away.

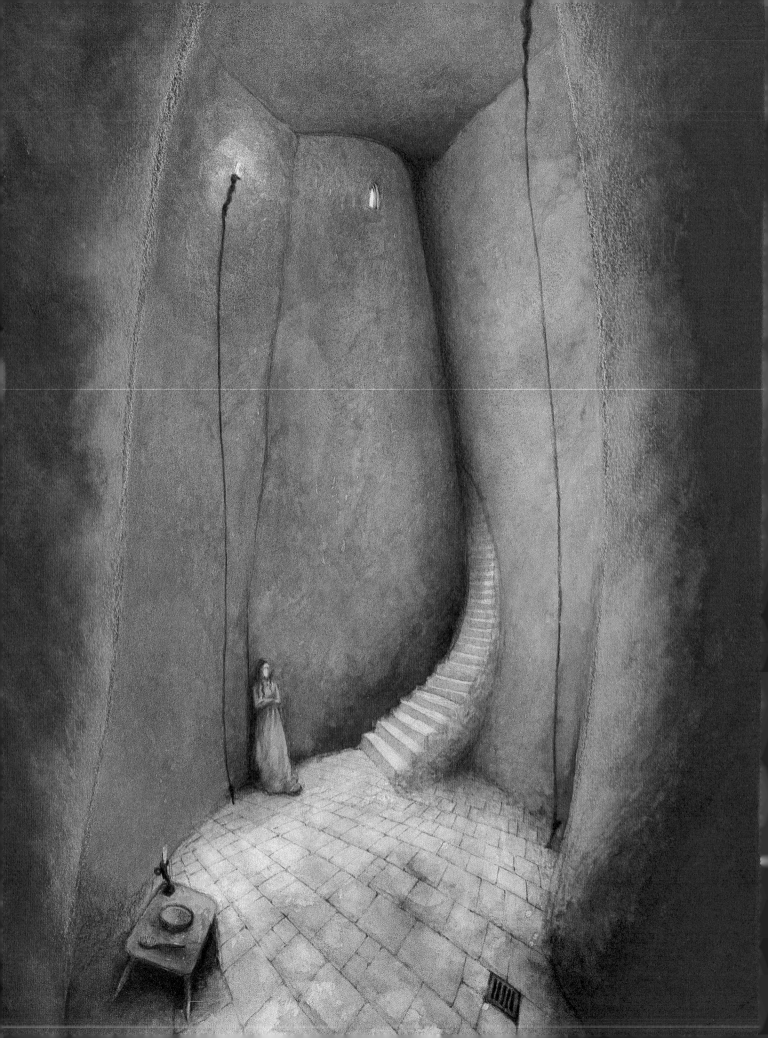

The uncle was furious at Phoebe for letting the bird escape. When word came that the prince would return after the next full moon, the old man feared he would be blamed for the loss. He sent his own guards to watch the royal garden and imprisoned Phoebe beneath the castle. There she would have stayed had it not been for the mysterious arrival of another bird, the River Flute.

What excitement there was when the bird sang out in its high, quivering voice! How the hunters shouted when they glimpsed it flashing down from tree limb to water!

Phoebe heard about the bird and sent a message to the uncle, offering to catch it for him. The old man knew the prince would reward him well for such a gift. He said to the girl, "Capture the River Flute for me, and you shall go free. But you must promise to return one day after the full moon. If you try to run away, I will find and punish you."

At dawn Phoebe set off, following the curve of the glittering river. Birds rushed up from the fields beside her. The forest was deep in song, inviting her in. But Phoebe kept her promise, traveling close to the water for several days in search of the River Flute. One afternoon she saw a dozen birds circling the edge of a field.

"Brothers, what is it?" she sang out to them.

"A hunter, a hunter," the birds cawed back.

Two dogs in the grass began to yelp. Phoebe followed them to their master. He was trapped in a hole, his clothes muddy and torn, his leg bloody. Phoebe worked quickly to free the hunter and bandaged his leg with her belt.

"Now you know how it feels to be caught," she said, eyeing the skins he carried.

The bearded hunter looked curiously at the girl and asked her why she was traveling alone. Phoebe told him about the lost bird, then all that had happened since the prince had left his people in the hands of his uncle. The hunter turned away. But when she spoke of the River Flute, he turned back quickly. "Let me search with you," he said.

They traveled together for days. The hunter
delighted in telling Phoebe the names of all the wild
birds. He taught her how to live off the land and
water; Phoebe taught him to love them. In her eyes he
saw the shining sky and river, the restless toss of the
trees. Each path they chose left another that the girl
longed to explore with her new friend. But each night
the moon grew rounder.

It was the evening of the full moon when Phoebe and the hunter heard a bird's long, flutey call. They rushed to the water's edge. The hunter quickly spread his bait and drew out his net.

The River Flute sang high above them. When it dove, its eyes burned gold and its wings flamed with color. Again and again it plunged toward the river, snatching the bait. Each time it escaped the hunter's net.

Then Phoebe whistled a high, rippling song and held
out her arm. The bird circled close to her and came to rest.
Cupping it in her hands, she felt its wild heart beating.

Suddenly she lifted both arms. "Fly! Fly! Fly!" she cried out.
The bird spiraled upward.

"What have you done?" her friend exclaimed. "We shall never
see the bird again!"

But Phoebe's face shone. "You might, for it is free now to return."

"What will you tell the prince's uncle?" the hunter persisted.
"When he learns you have freed the bird, do you think he will free you?"

Phoebe knew he would not. She warned her friend against returning with her, but he stayed by her side. They traveled through the night and at sunrise arrived at the castle. The prince's uncle met them, demanding at once to see the bird.

Phoebe opened her empty hands.

"She let it escape," her friend said softly.

The old man grew angry. "Do not expect mercy from me! You know the price!"

"She knows," the hunter said, his voice still soft.
"When my nephew the prince returns—"
"I have," the young man replied,
taking Phoebe's hand, "though I wear
a hunter's beard and clothes."

Then the prince began to set his kingdom in order. His uncle, having scorned mercy, did not dare to ask for it; as soon as darkness fell, he crept away from the castle. Phoebe returned to the garden.

The next morning the prince visited her.

"Tell me what you wish for, Phoebe," he said, "to be a keeper of birds or wife of a prince? If you choose to be my wife," he added gently, "both the birds and I shall be yours forever."

Phoebe held a small bird in her hands. Its heart beat as swiftly as her own. She lifted her arms, sending the bird aloft—but only as high as the flowering cage.

"I wish I could fly," she said.

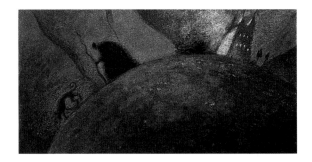

Not long after, Phoebe and the prince parted. The morning she left, the prince had the gate removed from the garden. Some birds flew off quickly; others stayed. But the prince's eyes were on Phoebe. From a high window he watched her follow the shimmering river, till she was out of sight.

His advisors said, "Forget her, my lord. You will never see that girl again."

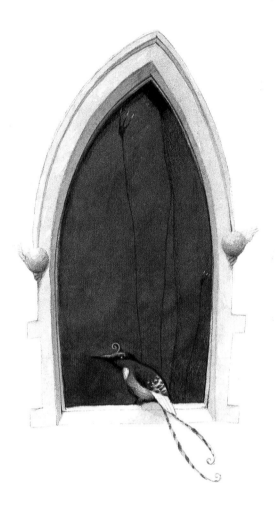

But the prince did not forget.
He knew that Phoebe was free to return.
And one day she might.